We're NOT so Different after all!

Story by LISSETTE LENT Illustrations by JESSICA FRAMPTON

This book is dedicated to my awesome kids. Andrew, Isabella, Noah and Maggie Hope;
I cannot tell you enough how much I love you all and feel blessed to be your mom.
Thank you for giving my life such purpose.

A special thanks to Stephen and all of my beloved family and friends. Thank you for your constant support, prayers and well wishes during this journey. To Maggie's amazing therapists throughout the years, you have been so instrumental in Maggie's development.

THANK YOU!

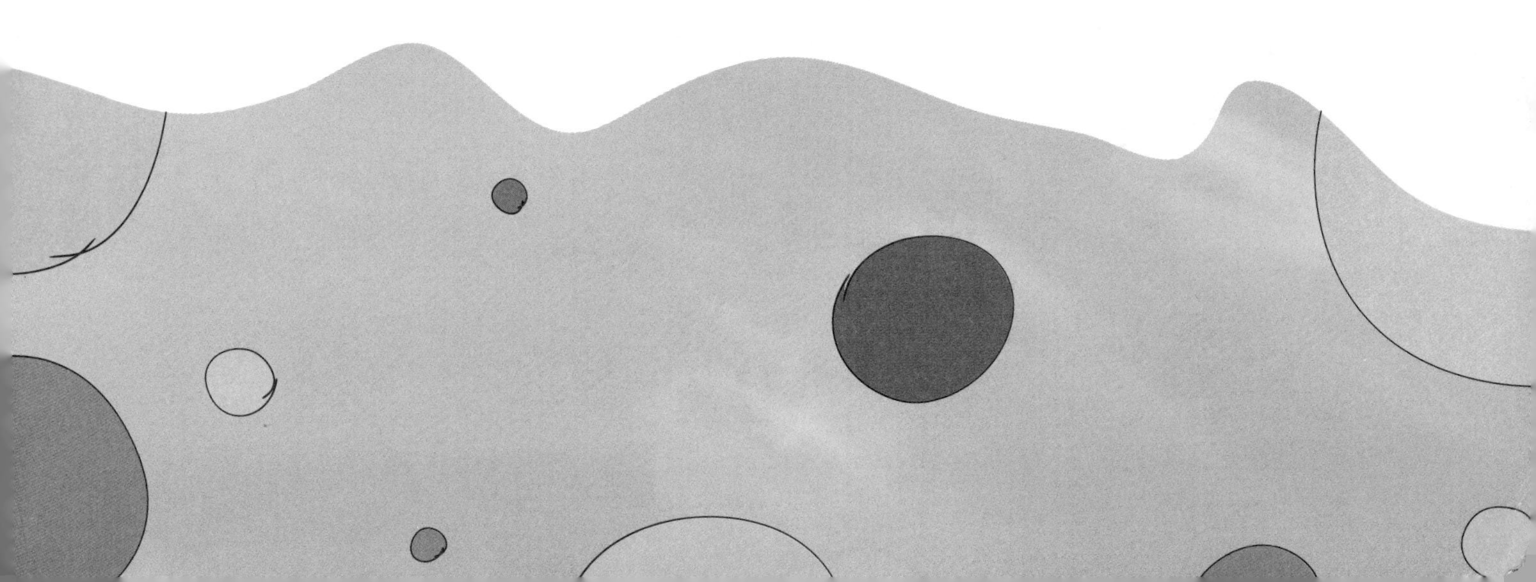

My name is Noah,
I'm a kid just like you.
I'm learning, I'm growing
and discovering, too.

Most other children
look just like me,
then there are others
that look and act differently.

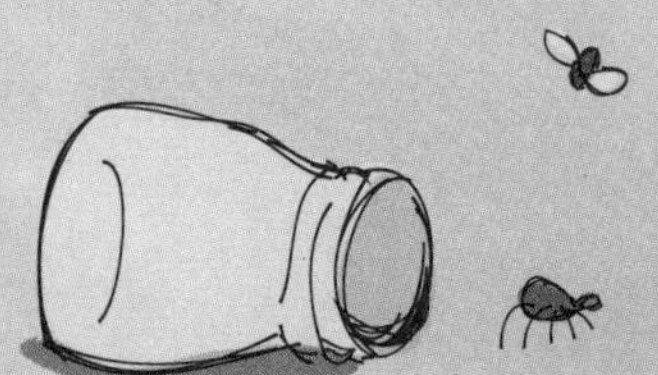

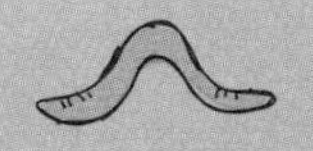

When someone looks different,
I get nervous - don't you?
I get scared, I get shy,
not sure what to do.

Mommy and Daddy say,
"Don't run away.
Every child just wants
friends and to play."

All kids have feelings and will get sad if I'm mean.
I must be brave and do the right thing.

I've learned this first hand
from my sister, you see.
It's time to meet her!
Her name is
MAGGIE!
We're NOT so different after all!

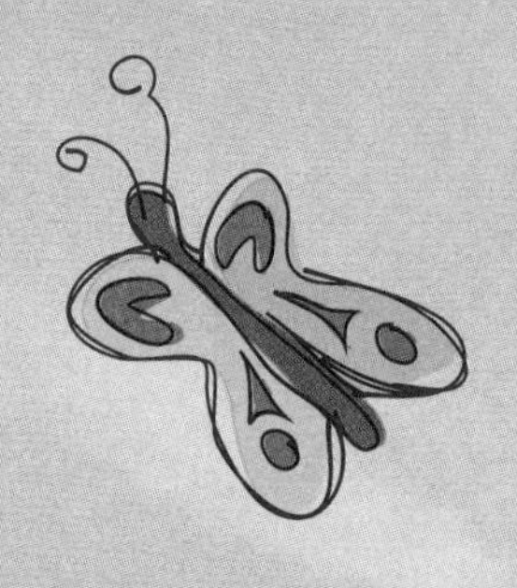

What are those glasses
she wears on her face?
They look kind of silly.
They look out of place.

But wait...

She has brown eyes.
She has brown hair.
She loves to snuggle
my teddy bear.

We're NOT so different after all!

Why does she wear
that hat on her head?
I don't like that she
wears it to bed.

But wait...

Sometimes I wear
funny hats, too.
I have them in black,
red, yellow and blue.

We're NOT so different after all!

It's strange that she can't
eat foods that are yummy.
What is that tube sticking
out of her tummy?

But wait...

One day she'll eat from her mouth, just like me. The veggies and fruits will make her happy.

We're NOT so different after all!

The wheelchair she sits in
doesn't seem very fun.
She can't kick a ball.
She can't walk or run.

But wait...

She loves to laugh,
be silly and play.
Bath time is her favorite
part of the day.

We're NOT so different after all!

She screams when she's happy
and talks with her hands.
It kind of scares me.
I don't understand.

But wait...

She has two arms,
two legs and a nose;
I counted ten fingers.
I counted ten toes.

We're NOT so different after all!

The braces on her chest
and her legs make me worry.
She moves so slow,
unable to hurry.

But wait...

As soon as the music
starts to play,
she loves to dance!
Get out of her way!

We're NOT so different after all!

It takes her so long
to learn simple stuff.
I don't understand
what makes things so tough.

But wait...

She loves to color
and draw in her book,
build castles in the sand,
and help mom and dad cook.

We're NOT so different after all!

Maggie has taught me to not be afraid.
We may all look different, but we are equally made.
It's okay to be curious, ask questions and smile.
You can even offer your help every once in a while.

So, mommies and daddies, it's all up to you.
Please talk to your kids, so they understand too.
When meeting new people, be friendly, be kind!
Chances are, a new friend you will find!

We're NOT so different after all!

Start the Conversation...

Most children look and act just like you; they like to ride their bikes and play at the park. They like to eat their favorite foods and spend time talking to friends. Sometimes you might see children that look and act differently. These children may have special needs or disabilities. A disability is something that may cause a person to be limited in certain things he or she can do. Sometimes their bodies don't look like your body or they do things that don't make sense to you. Some children are born with disabilities while others experience something in their life that causes that disability. This can affect them in many different ways. Some children need wheelchairs and walkers or even special tubes and machines to help them do everyday things. Just because someone may seem different, doesn't mean they don't enjoy doing all the things you enjoy. They want to have friends just like you do. We all have things that make us special and different from one another but our similarities outweigh our differences. Let's remember to treat everyone with kindness and compassion.

Questions and Answers

1. Have you ever met someone that you think looked or acted differently than you? When and where?

2. How did the way that person looked or acted make you feel? (curious, confused, happy, sad)

3. Why do you think you felt that way?

4. How did you treat that person?

5. What were some of the differences that you noticed?

6. What were some of the similarities that you noticed?

7. What can you do to make others feel included or accepted?

8. What are some of the ways that you can encourage your friends to treat others with kindness and compassion?

The next time you see someone that looks or acts differently, remember M.A.G.G.I.E!

Make a new friend

Accept them for who they are

Greet them with a smile

Get to know them by asking questions

Invite them to play with you

Educate and inspire others to act with kindness

Lissette met Stephen in 1996 and the couple started their family shortly after. In 2007, after deciding they were done having children, Lissette discovered she was pregnant with their fourth baby. At 17 weeks pregnant, the family was told some devastating news about their baby girl. Her brain, heart and kidneys were not forming properly. Throughout the pregnancy, the news only got worse. All of the facts and professional opinions pointed the family to very little hope. Doctors said that if their baby survived the pregnancy, she would need immediate surgery and she could have severe mental and physical disabilities. In those unsettling moments, Stephen and Lissette knew they had to step out of their despair, move forward and fight for hope. Maggie Hope was born on May 13, 2008, and was diagnosed with a rare genetic disorder called Trisomy 8 Mosaicism. After many prayers, surgeries and instrumental therapies, she defies the odds and continues to surpass her doctors' expectations. She brings joy and delight to everyone she encounters. Maggie's life is a beautiful display of strength and perseverance, and a perfect reflection of her name, *HOPE*.

Maggie Lent, 2015

Paul Yerrick Photography
paulyerrick.com

Red Glasses Productions launched RedGlasses.org in 2015 with a mission to bring awareness, acceptance and hope to the millions of families and children living with special needs. With a vision to partner with parents, teachers and community leaders as a catalyst for change, Founder Lissette Lent created a series of children's books featuring the real-life experiences of her own daughter, Maggie Hope (diagnosed with Trisomy 8 Mosaicism Syndrome). Through these books, Red Glasses Productions hopes to inspire a generation of parents and their children to better understand and embrace people that look and act differently.

To find out more about the Lent family and Red Glasses Productions, visit us at

www.redglasses.org